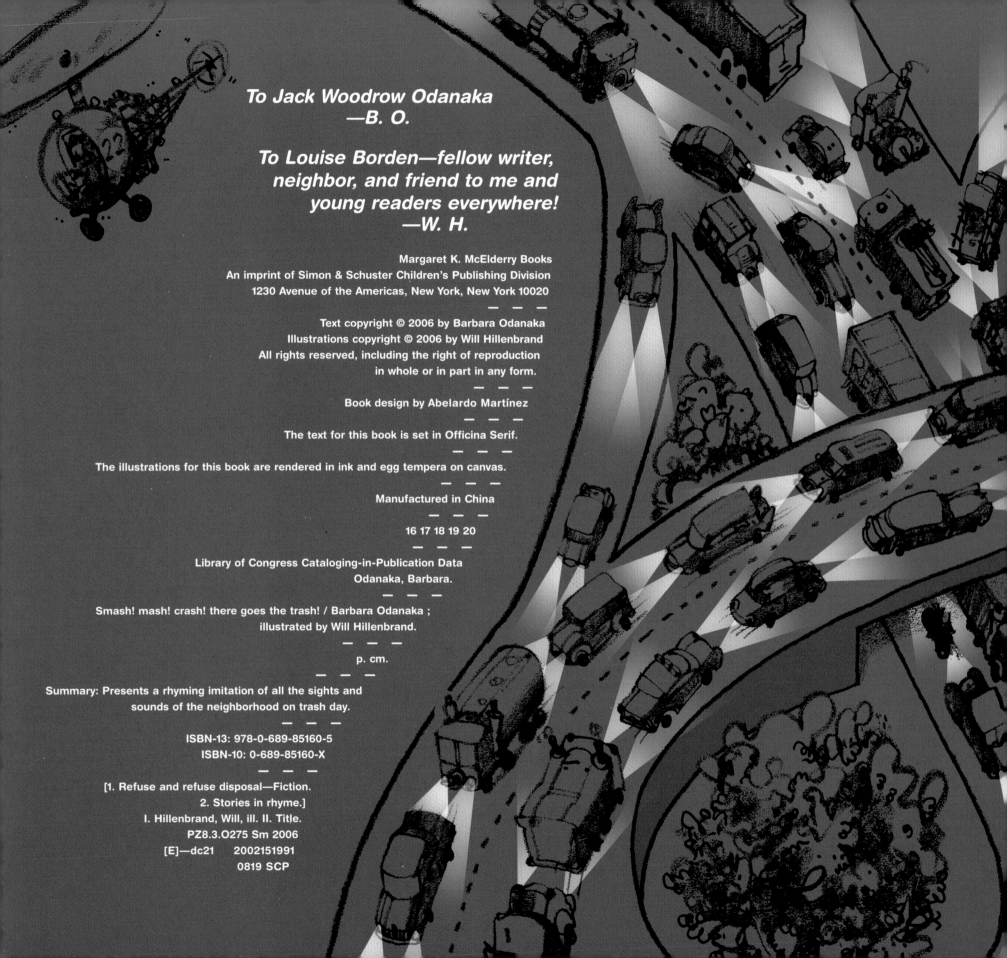

To Jack Woodrow Odanaka
—B. O.

To Louise Borden—fellow writer,
neighbor, and friend to me and
young readers everywhere!
—W. H.

Margaret K. McElderry Books
An imprint of Simon & Schuster Children's Publishing Division
1230 Avenue of the Americas, New York, New York 10020

— — —

Text copyright © 2006 by Barbara Odanaka
Illustrations copyright © 2006 by Will Hillenbrand

— — —

Book design by Abelardo Martínez

— — —

The text for this book is set in Officina Serif.

— — —

The illustrations for this book are rendered in ink and egg tempera on canvas.

— — —

Manufactured in China

— — —

16 17 18 19 20

— — —

Library of Congress Cataloging-in-Publication Data
Odanaka, Barbara.

— — —

Smash! mash! crash! there goes the trash! / Barbara Odanaka ;
illustrated by Will Hillenbrand.

— — —

p. cm.

— — —

Summary: Presents a rhyming imitation of all the sights and
sounds of the neighborhood on trash day.

— — —

ISBN-13: 978-0-689-85160-5
ISBN-10: 0-689-85160-X

— — —

[1. Refuse and refuse disposal—Fiction.
2. Stories in rhyme.]
I. Hillenbrand, Will, ill. II. Title.
PZ8.3.O275 Sm 2006
[E]—dc21   2002151991
0819 SCP

SMASH! MASH! CRASH!

THERE GOES THE TRASH!

Barbara Odanaka

illustrated by Will Hillenbrand

Margaret K. McElderry Books
New York London Toronto Sydney

Lifting,
loading,

squooshing,
squashing,
squeezing trash bags
to a pulp.

Run to the window—
feel the rumble?

Listen!

Hear it groan and grumble?

Down the street—hey, look, it's there!

Truck just chomped a broken chair.

Stinky diapers?
Coffee grounds?
Load it UP and
smash it DOWN.

Workers working
all day long.
Massive muscles,
oh so strong.

Greasy gloves . . . sticky boots . . . stains a-plenty on their suits.

Gooey, gloppy.

Slimy, sloppy.

Truck's a rolling bug buffet.

Flies a-buzzin'

by the dozen—

lapping up that cheese soufflé.

Black smoke belches.
Motor drones.
Crunching last night's
turkey bones.

Melon rinds . . .
moldy bread . . .
toss 'em in and forge ahead!

Crushing,
cramming,
screeching,
slamming,

garbage trucks

R-R-R-ROAR

away.

Wave good-bye.
Now *we'll* try:
SMASH!
MASH!
CRASH!

Come on, let's play!